REGAINING THE THRONE

Regaining the Throne

P.R. Allen Garcia

ONION RIVER PRESS

Onion River Press

89 Church Street

Burlington, VT 05401

info@onionriverpress.com

www.onionriverpress.com

ISBN: 978-1-966607-25-0

Library of Congress Control Number: 2025913130

AUTHOR'S NOTE

For many years, I've had a special place in my heart for Ireland and am lucky enough to have had a great-great grandfather born there. The places mentioned in this story are real, such as the small town of Cashel. The Rock of Cashel is a medieval complex that contains a cathedral, castle, and a round tower, among other ancient things. History states that this was the site where the last king of Munster was converted to Christianity by St. Patrick. Many people refer to the place as simply 'the Rock'.

Tipperary is a county and a town in southern Ireland. Meath is a county north of Dublin and is the site of the Hill of Tara where you can also find the Stone of Destiny, which was the ancient coronation place for kings of Ireland. The Well of the White Cow exists, as does the Mound of Hostages.

I'm not good at setting dates as time just seems to flow for me, but for this modern magical fairy tale, I'll say that it is set around 2010. Yes, the time there ebbs and flows like a river that has seemingly quiet, still, deep waters and then around a bend, rapids.

The Emerald Isle has a mystical, magical presence for me and is famous for an untold number of myths and legends as well as its poignant history. I hope that my magical creatures and occurrences only add to this enchanted isle.

I want to thank Beth Cole for her gentle suggestions on how to improve this story—a truly beautiful friend. And my son, Shan, who has helped me with my computer issues, which had me stymied.

IRISH VOCABULARY

Aye: yes
Cad: scoundrel
Chancer: a person who takes risks
Daidí: daddy
Eegit: a foolish or stupid person
Feck: f**k
Flute: an idiot
Garda: policeman
Halla an Bhaile: town hall
Handfasting: a ceremony where the hands are tied together; a binding together
Maimeó: grandmother
Mo: my, mine
Ossified: very drunk
Puca: spirit or ghost
Scuttered: drunk
Uilleann pipes: Irish bagpipes
Ye / yer: you / your

PROLOGUE

Cashel, Ireland

An old woman, wearing black, with a shawl wrapped around her shoulders, is sitting on a stone bench next to the ancient castle's burial site. "It's her; she's finally come!" she whispers to herself. "The prophesy will finally come true, and my days of waiting will soon be over."

ONE

"Good afternoon. I've just arrived from the States, and for some reason I think traveling by train in your beautiful country will be exciting. This pamphlet fell at my feet, and I was wondering if you could tell me how to get to the town of Cashel, please?"

"Good day to you, too, lass. You've come to the correct station. This is the Hueston station, and the trip will take you a wee bit more than an hour," says the man at the ticket office.

He hands me my ticket and directs me to the correct platform, and soon I'm on my way. For some reason, I think my ancestors are guiding me towards this place, and my mind starts imagining a new storyline for a future book. The train stops in Thurles, and from there I take a taxi to Cashel.

I've finally made it to the small town of Cashel, south of Dublin, and I am now at the Rock of Cashel, an ancient, historical site. What am I doing here? I wish I knew, but something has drawn me to this place, almost like a magical siren, drawing and pulling me across the big pond. I know I have Irish ancestors, but I've never been to the Emerald Isle before now, although it has been in my dreams, so much more lately—at least I think I've been dreaming about Ireland. Now, I have no idea what has had me asking how to get from Dublin to Cashel; perhaps a wee leprechaun whispering to me in my dreams? No, I'll not be mentioning that to the Irish or they'll kick me off their beautiful isle, I'm sure.

I am Tara Connors from Vermont—a rather successful author of children's books—and now am reflecting if I have actually lost all sense of reason. I have never done anything so calculatingly illogical as this trip. I mentioned my dreams of late about Ireland, but my computer screen saver has only had photos of Ireland popping up for the last month and that is truly weird and, dare I say, spooky.

I'm outside walking along a road, pulling my suitcase, when I see some very big ruins. I pull out the pamphlet and see that this place is called the Rock of Cashel or St. Patrick's Rock. It looks like a church but also a bit like a castle. I walk up towards the ruins, and near the castle or cathedral is a burial site where I start looking at the stones. Suddenly, I glance up and see the clouds open and a sunbeam seems to land on one of the ancient stones. I make my way over to a very simple slab with some strange markings on it. I bend over, touch it, and it is warm and seems to vibrate, sending pulsating energy up my arm. I must be more tired than I thought, or I'm hallucinating, as it also looks like a white dove circling above my head.

I'll come back another day once I've rested. I need to find a place to stay and something to eat before I collapse.

I head back to the path and see an old woman sitting on a bench nearby, so I go over and introduce myself.

"Good afternoon, ma'am, I'm Tara Connors and I just arrived from Dublin, and I was hoping that you might know of a good place to stay near here."

She says that her name is Ole Annie, and she hands me a stone with a carving on it and tells me to go the O'Riley Pub and ask for Patrick, that he'll set me up. I thank her and make my way into town.

I finally locate the pub that Ole Annie mentioned, and when I walk in, there are three men behind the bar, two with bright red hair and one with black. I ask for Patrick, and the tallest one, with black hair and emerald eyes, comes over but the other two are right behind him. I mention Ole Annie, and they laugh, but when I hand Patrick the stone, he looks at me strangely. "And what would ya be wantin'?" he says in a rather unpleasant voice.

I tell him that I'm looking for a place to rent for a couple of months: a small cottage, if possible, away from others. I tell them that I'm Tara Conners, a writer and my computer forced me to come to Ireland. The three guys laugh out loud and one of them says; "Sure, and that's a real thing."

Patrick says he knows of a place but it's a bit late now. I can have a room above the pub for the night, and he'll take me to see it in the morning.

"I'm Finn; tar liom. Sorry, miss, that means 'follow me'." He picks up my suitcase and leads me upstairs. He shows me a room with a bath attached and tells me that they serve food downstairs as it's a pub.

"Thank you, Finn. Why did you laugh at me when I mentioned that my computer forced me to come here? It's the truth."

"Miss, I'm a computer geek, and nothing like that has ever happened to me, so I hope you'll excuse my inability to believe that," Finn says. "Unless of course you have a computer that has AI, which I don't think exists yet."

"Well, I guess I'll just have to show you then."

"That would be a fine thing—perhaps tomorrow," replies Finn.

I go downstairs after resting and cleaning myself up. The pub is busy. I see Finn drawing beer; Patrick is over by a window chatting with some men. The other man sees me and comes over.

"Well, Ms. Conners, I'm glad to see ya. I'm Liam. Would ya be wanting something to eat? We've got shepard's pie for tonight's special," he explains as he shows me to a small table.

I ask if that's a typical dish, and he replies that it is and a very tasty one at that. Liam sits down and starts to chat about the town and things to do. He also mentions that he loves to cook and that maybe we can get together another time to talk about Ireland's typical dishes. I love how friendly he is and easy to talk with as I've never been able to talk so easily with men before. I'm wondering about the atmosphere here and the changes I feel happening to me.

* * *

I'm up early the next morning, and it's obvious that the pub isn't open to the public yet, but I hear noise in the kitchen and head back where I think that I will find Liam. Instead I find a girl who appears to be a little younger than me. I introduce myself, and she shyly says her name is Bevin.

"Is it alright if I'm in the kitchen? I don't want to cause any problems. That man Patrick wasn't very nice yesterday."

We strike up a conversation, and I ask if I may help her knead the scones they'll be serving this morning, then I work on the bread dough that has a while to go. I ask if they also serve muffins, but she says they don't. I tell her I have a recipe for morning muffins that uses carrots, apples, and raisins and I'll write it out for her if she'd like it.

"Well Bevin, if I'm not being too forward, what does your name mean? I've never met anyone with that name."

"Oh, well, I'm not surprised as it is an Irish name, after all. It means white lady. I think me mam was a bit tired after giving birth, or so she said, and when she saw me, she mentioned how white I was. Me daidí was a bit tipsy, so he thought that was what me mam wanted for me name," Bevin tells me.

"That is a beautiful story! It is a great name for you as you are very fair and quite lovely. What can you tell me about typical Irish food? I can't wait to try some."

"There is a lot, and it's really good and filling. Of course our Irish stew is well known, but we also have colcannon, Guinness pie, bangers and mash, rhubarb tart, mashed peas, boxty, scones, bannock, pasties, champ, and barmbrack. Those are just a few, but then each county has its own specialty," Bevin laughs.

"Wow, I hope I get to try a lot of those things. Do you make most of them here?"

"Most of them, but Patrick's brother Liam is really the chef, here and I'm more of the baker," she clarifies. "My sister Rose loves to cook as well, but she doesn't have much time. I'm sure she would love to meet you."

"I'd love to meet her. What does she do?"

"She runs a big hotel outside of town and is a workaholic. Maybe I can get her to start taking some time off to meet a new friend," Bevin says.

We're laughing about the strange foods each of us eat when Patrick comes in to see what the laughter is all about.

"Good day to ye lovely ladies." He smiles. "Bevin, are you telling tall tales to our guest?" He scowls.

"Oh no, sir. I'd never do that!" Bevin shrinks away and takes some of the scones out of the oven.

"Well, aren't you just the sardonic person in the morning! It does not become you being nasty this early!" I go over and give Bevin a hug and thank her for the tea and our early morning talk. "I would really like to talk to you again and hope we can become friends." I stomp out past Patrick, bumping his shoulder as I go.

"And where do you think you're off to?" Patrick smirks as he looks me up and down.

"Enjoying the view, are you?" I snap at him. Of course, I had forgotten that I'd come down for a cup of coffee or tea and only had on my purple and green satin and lace robe over my sleeping shorts and tank top. "Forget about the cottage," I snap. "I'll find one on my own, and as soon as I shower and change, I'll be out of your hair!"

I stomp around in my room for a few minutes, trying to calm down before I head for the shower. I do love their thick, soft, and fluffy towels that I wrap around myself. I'm heading towards the bed when there's a knock on the door. I expect it's Bevin, so I open it and tell the person to come in. When I turn around, it's Patrick with a huge smile on his face.

"And here I thought you were angry with me." Patrick laughs.

I shriek and grab my towel and shout, "I thought it was Bevin, not you, you perverted ogre. Get out!"

"Guess you're still upset then." He smiles. "Well, it's a good thing that I've come to apologize, and hope you'll accept my invitation to breakfast as a way to make it up to you. Ye see, it is most unusual to have a guest in the kitchen, let alone help with food prep. Ye see, Bevin is dear to us but ever so shy, so I was shocked she took to you so fast. Truly, I was only thinking of protecting her. So, my dear colleen, I sincerely apologize and hope you'll permit me to show you the place Ole Annie wants you to see."

"I . . . I guess that will be alright, and I accept your apology, but if you don't leave immediately, I'll be throwing something at you!"

Patrick laughs and leaves and says that he'll be waiting downstairs for me.

I go over and lock the door and get dressed in a hurry, then I make my bed and finish packing the few things I took out last night. I have a backpack that I use to carry special things, like sunscreen and a raincoat as well as my water bottle and a can of mace.

TWO

I walk downstairs with my suitcase, which Patrick takes and places behind the bar. "Follow me then." We head outside where he puts my backpack in his car then comes around and opens my door. We don't travel very far when he stops at The Bakehouse. He takes me upstairs where there is a small, cozy café. As we eat breakfast, he tells me that Ole Annie said that we can't see the cottage until three and then asks me how I came to Cashel in particular.

"It's rather difficult to explain—well not difficult but rather strange as it felt like something was pulling me to Ireland. I mean, like one day I opened my computer and it was on a page about flights to Ireland and I had never googled that. I don't believe in ghosts but that started me thinking that something weird was going on. That was the last thing that convinced me that I needed to come. Once I landed in Dublin, I went to the train station where a brochure for Cashel fell at my feet—I mean it literally floated to my feet, but there was no breeze, so I took that as a sign to come here. The Rock drew me, also like a magnet, so I immediately went to see what was pulling me, but it was at a burial site that I saw and sensed an astonishingly strange phenomenon. A ray of sunlight broke through the clouds and was shining on an unmarked grave, and when I touched the stone, it was warm. Then I felt something like vibrations going up my arm. I wasn't scared; if anything it felt comforting, like a warm, embracing welcome. After that, a white dove followed me around.

"It's okay if you want to laugh at me or think I'm crazy, but please don't mention it to anyone and I won't bother you anymore. I just want a place to stay that's comfortable and warm for two or three months, maybe more. I don't know what Ole Annie saw or why she gave me that stone, but she seemed sincere, and I hope to visit with her again while I'm here. She smiled at me, and as funny as it sounds, I felt connected to her. I'm sure she can tell me a lot about the Rock."

Patrick just stares at me with a quizzical look on his face. He finally says, "Let me show you some of our village; then after lunch, I'll show you this cottage off of Golden Road and see what you think."

After we finish eating, he drives me around the town and points out different stores, eateries, and historical places and then asks me to show him the burial site at the Rock.

He looks at the grave that I indicate and asks if I am positive that this is the correct one. "Are you sure that this is the site? After all, there are several exactly like this one." he snaps at me.

I state emphatically that it is. I touch it and can feel vibrations. Patrick reaches down and touches it also but doesn't say anything. I ask if he knows who is buried in this site, and he says, "According to legend, it could be the last king of Ireland and his wife. He was buried in an unmarked grave so vandals wouldn't steal it or desecrate and scatter his remains. No one can be truly sure which grave is his unless it is dug up, and we're a wee bit superstitious about disturbing the dead," he retorts.

"Look, I'm sorry if I've done something wrong, but I have no idea why you would be angry with me. Don't worry about showing me the place Ole Annie mentioned; I'll find someone else. I don't want to impose on you any longer."

We head back to his pub for lunch and so I can collect my things.

"Look," Patrick starts, "I apologize again—and it's gettin' a bit repetitive. You aren't the first person who Ole Annie has sent to us, but you are the first she has had me wait to show the place. I have no idea what she's up to, and it ticks me off. I'm sorry if I've been a wee bit short with ye."

Finally, he takes me about a kilometer outside the town to where there's a rutty lane leading to a small stone cottage surrounded by dried-up flowers and I think herbs. It sits nestled in front of a forest; on one side is a little brook and the cottage is all by itself. Patrick says that it is an ancient place but has been updated a bit on the inside.

When he gets to a fancy, thick wooden door that is carved with a fascinating scene, I am awe struck—it's so beautiful. And then I wonder how it opens as there is no key hole or doorknob. He pulls out the stone that Ole Annie gave me and hands it to me. I now realize it's a heavy piece of wood, and I place it in part of the carving without thinking, and the door swings open. I look at him, astounded, and all he says is that it is a little Irish magic and a very unique door; in fact, it works on both the front and back doors. "Guard your piece securely," he says. He shows me inside and starts to open the wooden shutters so light can come in. It is pretty much one room with a fireplace on one side, and the kitchen on the other end with a pantry next to it. There's a back door, and next to that is a modern stacked washer and dryer, a bathroom with a claw foot tub with a shower attachment, and then a closet. The rest of the place is open, with a table and four chairs, a queen-size bed, and a love seat and two comfy chairs in front of the fireplace. The kitchen has a small refrigerator, but there's an old-fashioned water pump for the stone sink. There's no phone, but I have my cell—although I will buy one here with a local number and save my U.S. one for my publisher. I love it all. It's so eclectic, just like me.

When I step out the back door into the garden, I feel a sunbeam hit me and it makes me laugh, throw up my arms, and twirl around and around, and I could swear that even the dried-up flowers seemed to dance around me. Soon the whole yard and cottage are basking in sunshine. I see a white dove again, and I wonder if it is the same one that I saw before but that seems silly. She flies down and lights on an old wooden bench.

Patrick is frozen in the doorway, glancing at his phone. I ask him how much the rent is, and after a minute, he says, "It's only a hundred euros a month, but the person who stays here has to remain for a minimum of six months."

I can't believe my ears or my luck. I run to him and hug him and say, "I'll take it! It feels like I've been here before; in fact it kind of looks like one of the screen savers I saw on my computer. I can't wait to show that to Finn." I ask where I need to go to sign the contract or lease or whatever. I'm so excited and happy that I almost forget to ask him the address or name of the cottage so I can get things delivered. Patrick says it's called The Queen's Hideaway. He asks if I want to stay there right away or wait a while.

"Of course I want to move in immediately!"

He says that the place was cleaned and stocked today, which surprises me. He says that there is a bicycle in the shed out back that I can use as well. I can't wait to meet the owner or realtor, but for now, I just want to sit in the back garden and breathe. I grab Patrick's hand and shake it, a bit surprised at the jolt I feel, but then I thank him for all he's done and say that I owe him big time and if there's anything I can do for him, just let me know.

"Aye, we'll see about that. I expect you'll be like the others—in and out in a day or so. None have lasted more than that. I doubt that you're anyone special," he states.

"Oh, but you see, you're wrong! Each and everyone is special and unique; all you have to do is genuinely look at them." I almost swallow my tongue. Where did those words come from? I'm never so outspoken.

"Good day to ya, colleen." Patrick grunts as he leaves.

I actually hide away for a few days. Whoever stocked the cottage left me enough to eat for a week, and I'm in no hurry to leave this sanctuary. I find great comfort and peace both inside and out of this special place. Back in Vermont, I was having a dry spell. I love my children's books and all the little creatures I created with the wild animals, but I needed a break. I think I want to do something different. I've always been a loner, and I've been reflecting on my life. I need a change. I've come to realize that God has protected me throughout my life without me giving Him the credit due. I never went to wild parties, drank nor did drugs. Most people think of me as introverted and boring—if they ever think of me at all. Something is telling me that it's time for me to change. This place reminds me of Vermont, so green and beautiful.

THREE

I'm in the garden, sitting on an old wooden bench, when I hear something near the tree line. Then some of the flowers start swaying and out step two little kittens. They appear to be several months old, and I believe they are of the Manx breed and they are calico. They head straight towards me, sit down in front of me, tip their heads to the side and look at me, then start rubbing my ankles. I pet them both and rub behind their ears then ask if they would like a bit of milk. Both answer with purrs. I take them inside and give them what I have. "Would the two of you like some tuna fish to go with the milk?" They stop drinking and sit down and look at me with what appear to be smiles. I laugh and say, "Of course, now who wouldn't like tuna fish? I think you guys need names—unless you belong somewhere else and just came visiting. I shall have to ask around if someone is missing you two, but I hope you are here to stay. I think that you, little one, shall be Truffle, and you shall be Carmel. Are those names fine with you two?" I hear purrs but it may be because they are waiting for the tuna fish, which I set down for them. "You two realize that I shall need to get you some things if you are going to grace me with your company." It looks like a ride into town is in my near future.

I decide, on my ride into town, to go by the O'Riley Pub to find out about the lease, as I don't have Patrick's number nor have I bought a new phone. I don't want to be arrested for trespassing, so I need to sign the lease and pay my rent. I also want to see if a local store will deliver groceries to the cottage. I'm planning on getting a phone here, and I would like to get one for Ole Annie if she doesn't have one, but I need to talk to her first or Patrick, at least. I think that she may be able to tell me all about the Rock, the cottage, and Ireland as well. I feel a special draw towards her. She has such a comforting personality, almost like a long lost relative.

Patrick isn't at the pub, but his brother Liam is in the kitchen, and he says that he has the paperwork in the office for me to sign and that I can leave the rent money with him. He gives me a list of phone numbers that I might find useful, but when I inquire as to who the owner is, he says it has to remain anonymous but that it's a little convoluted as the cottage belongs to a group and has for centuries. I say that I'd like to know who to thank as I love it. I also want to know if pets are allowed as two kittens have shown up. He assures me that there is no problem and the group will be happy to know that animals have shown up. I tell him that there is also a white dove that seems to make its home there but I don't know what to feed it. "Well, actually, I think that it's the one I saw at the Rock on the day I arrived."

I'm off to the store for kitty food and some wild bird seed, but before I go too crazy with food supplies, I ask someone if they can deliver, and they confirm that they do. They also sell cell phones (or as they inform me politely, mobiles) so I buy two, and as they are setting them up, I buy my groceries. When I go to pay, I ask them to deliver them, so they ask the address and I say the Queen's Hideaway. I hear gasps and people saying; "That's her. She's the one." I feel strange but everyone is smiling and bowing their heads, so I smile and bow mine back to them. Perhaps it's a tradition here; I shall have to ask Ole Annie.

FOUR

A few more days go by, and I start seeing more animals. I am having an early morning cup of tea with Truffle and Caramel when I spy some deer at the edge of the trees. They come over to the brook to drink, and then a white deer appears and seems to stare at me before she, too, drinks. She is breathtakingly beautiful. I decide to call her Moonbeam, and I talk to her when she comes by.

I spend most mornings weeding some, but I find that there aren't many weeds to pull and all the dried-up flowers are now alive and blooming. I tell the kittens that this place is mysterious as what appeared to be long dead is now alive and blooming. I enjoy talking to the kittens as they truly seem to listen. Sometimes I see some weeds in the evening, but when I come out in the morning to work, they are gone. I laughingly tell my kittens that the garden fairies must be helping me.

I ride to town to find a café that has Wi-Fi to check my email and update my publisher about my next book. Truth be told, I am having such a beautiful stay here that I haven't been doing a lot of writing, but I am excited about doing a project about God's little creatures here and of course my garden fairies. I also go back to the Rock several times as it calls to me. I have talked to Ole Annie many times, and now I offer her the phone, which surprises her and seems to please her. I show her how to use it and the numbers that I have programmed in for her.

"Well, colleen, this is a surprise, but I do enjoy our visits, and if you ever need anything now you can call me," Ole Annie laughs.

"Ya know that the Rock was the traditional site for the Kings of Munster, and while it looks like a castle, it is not. It is believed that our beloved Saint Patrick baptized the king here. There is a spring inside, and it's said that Saint Patrick used water from that for the baptism. The king eventually ceded the site to the Catholic Church," Ole Annie narrates.

* * *

One day, I am sitting at Morelli's, a café and restaurant, having a cappuccino and working with my publisher—they have Wi-Fi for their customers—when a good-looking man comes up and asks if I am Tara Connors. I confirm that I am, and he introduces himself as Antonio Morelli and asks if he can buy me a cup of coffee. I point to my finished cappuccino, so he calls one of his servers and asks him to bring two more out to the table.

We talk for a while, and then he asks me to have dinner with him and not to worry about changing as what I'm wearing is fine. I accept then head over to the Rock to commune with the great place. It seems to infuse me with strong feelings and a warmth. I wish I knew what was happening—it seems almost magical, but I'm too agnostic to believe in that. I also wish that I could touch more of its rooms, but they are roped off as it is a national historic place. My white dove, that I named Paz, finds me here and perches on my shoulder as I walk around the place.

Antonio and I have a lovely meal, and he tells me the story of how his family came to live here, plus about his Italian family as well. He's a charming man, intelligent and really handsome with a winning smile. Of course, he intrigues me with stories of ghosts, fairies, and even the púca. He then tells me that he will drive me back to the cottage as he doesn't want me to be accosted by any of Ireland's mystical creatures, and he puts my bike in the back of his SUV. During our drive, Antonio says, "I want you to know that I have a bit of a reputation that I'm trying to live down. Everyone here thinks I bounce from one woman to another and I won't deny that I enjoy female company but what I'm really looking for is a good friend, nothing more. I hope you'll let me take you, Rose, and Bevin to a few interesting sites so we can all get better acquainted."

"Antonio, I would love that. I don't think that I've ever had a man friend other than my brothers, and that's not really the same. I have never understood why men and women can't be just friends. I accept your offer and will mention it to my new friends."

It takes a little bit longer than normal for the drive as he's never been to this cottage and the turnoff is not easy to spot.

Antonio is just putting my bike up against the house when another car comes pulling up, and out jumps Patrick.

"Tara, we have to talk immediately!" he snaps. "Antonio, get lost."

"What?" I spit out, but Antonio laughs. "You've some nerve! Antonio, thank you for a lovely evening, and I apologize for this imprudent, nescient, unmannered man."

"I'll call you," replies Antonio as he kisses my hand.

"I wouldn't if I were you!" snarls Patrick.

I stomp into the cottage and whip around as Patrick comes in and smiles at me. "What in the world has gotten into you? Are you sick, is someone hurt, is Ole Annie okay?"

"What are ye talking about?" asks Patrick.

"'We have to talk 'immediately?' You were extremely rude to Antonio—need I say more?"

"Ye wouldn't know, but my little brother, Liam, saw you at Morelli's in the afternoon having coffee with him, then Finn tells me you were still there this early evening having dinner with him, and I'm thinking that no one told you that he's a world-class player, a chancer; he bounces from one woman to the next all the time. Has for years."

"Are you ossified or scuttered? Yes, I know that means drunk, thanks to my vocabulary lessons with Ole Annie. That's the only reason I can come up with that makes any sense. And just what am I to you to have your brothers spying on me?"

"We're not spying on ye. They just happened to see you and mentioned it to me, and now I'm asking you: What's Antonio to you?"

"Well, let me think! None of your fecking business. I only met him today, so how can he be more than a very nice, polite man?" I hardly recognize myself—I've never talked to anyone like this and certainly never a man. Our voices have been rising since we got inside and *bam—bam*! I screech and jump into Patrick's arms and just as quickly back out.

"What happened? What was that?"

We both look around to see that the front and back doors have opened and slammed shut. I go to open the front door to kick Patrick out but it won't open. I stomp to the back door and surprise; It won't open either!

"What did you do? Are you an evil wizard or something? I want you out of here now; I am so angry with you, I don't want to see you! Leave!"

"Well, now, there's a wee bit of a problem, isn't there; the doors won't open." And he starts laughing. "Did you know that when you're fighting mad, your hair practically glows red?"

"It does not!"

"Oh, but it does! A beautiful Irish red."

"I'm blonde, or are you blind as well as a flute?" I call him Irish slang for a foolish person.

"I surmise that you don't look in the mirror much, do ye? Ye may have been a blonde when you arrived, but you've gradually become a redhead," he says.

I run to the bathroom and look in the only mirror in the cottage. I have become a redhead! But when I look closer there seems to be a circle of blonde around the top of my head—strange.

I walk back to where Patrick is but don't say anything. I don't know what to make of the things that have happened to me here in Ireland. I feel at home, happy and strangely safe, except for this crazy man in my cottage.

Finally, Patrick says, "I apologize for bursting in on your romantic evening; I was a real fool." Then he looks down at the floor, like a scolded little boy, but I think I catch a smirk and that ticks me off. I remain quiet, and he looks up still smirking, and I lunge at him with my hand raised ready to slap that look off his face. He grabs my hand and jerks me to him and kisses me.

"Ay! Ohhhh!" I didn't mean to moan, but he's one great kisser! Finally, I snap out of it and push away from him, and when I do, I hear the door opening. Dang, it's magic or fairies or something else, I don't know. But I push Patrick out the door, shouting, "I don't know what you think you are doing, but it's best if you leave right now."

He replies, "I'll leave, but I'm not going to apologize for that kiss. I've wanted to do that since the day I met you, and just so you know, I have ne'er felt that way before. Perhaps this moment is not the best time to ask you for a date, but I want to know everything about you my *bean álainn* (beautiful woman). You are a very special person to me and FYI for the whole town."

"Your timing stinks! Go away!" I shut the door and take a deep breath. "Well, you two didn't help me much, did you?" Truffle and Caramel are stretched out on the bed, completely relaxed and purring, and I can almost swear they are smiling.

FIVE

I stomp back and forth for several minutes and completely forget to listen for Patrick's car leaving. I decide a wee bit of Jameson's single malt might help calm me down. I'm just getting a glass down when there's a soft knock on the door. I stomp over and throw it open, ready to lambaste Patrick, but he's standing there with this beautiful bouquet of white flowers in his hand.

He sighs then says, "I'm an eegit, and I don't know what got into me. I really have never done anything like this before, and I beg yer forgiveness. Please, Tara, forgive me!"

Oh, just great! Now what am I going to do?

"You know you truly drive me crazy? One minute you're nice and polite and the next hollering and giving orders; I don't know what to expect from you or who you are. Oh Lord, help me! Come in." I step aside.

"I was just going to have a drink; would you like one?"

"Aye, I would, thank you. Here, these are for you; they are moon flowers and open at night."

I thank him, take the flowers and put them in a mason jar. I suggest we sit in the backyard, and I carry the flowers with me as he brings the glasses. Of course I know that they are from the gardens around the cottage, but it's the thought that counts, right?

We sit on the old wooden bench, and I put the flowers on a flat stone. The kittens decide to come out and play, running in and out of the flowers in the garden. Then they start chasing a ball. Patrick and I watch them awhile before he decides to break the silence.

"Are you happy here?" he asks.

"Yes, incredibly happy. In fact, this feels more like home than where I come from. Don't get me wrong, I love Vermont, yet being here somehow has a deeper meaning. Ole Annie has told me a great deal about the people here, and everyone has been very nice. I love it here, and I love the people. Ole Annie feels like long lost family. I feel I can count Bevin as a new friend as well as her sister Rose, who I've met a few times. Actually, I want to take them to Dublin before the music festival, to do some shopping as they know where to go—if they can get time off. Antonio has offered to take the three of us to the coast, and I can't wait to see the St. George's Channel."

Patrick grinds his teeth and sighs. "Please, colleen, be careful with him. You mean a great deal to me, and I don't want to see you hurt."

"Why, Mr. O'Riley, that is very nice of you to be concerned, but can you explain why I mean so much to you?"

"Truly, I wish I could, but I'm at a loss to understand it myself; it must be the fairies." He sighs.

"Well, that 'truly' doesn't answer my question at all." I look around but don't see Moonbeam. "I had hoped you might be able to see my nightly visitor, but perhaps it's best if you leave now."

"What? What visitor? Are you insinuating that you have a lover?"

I dive for him, ready to slap his face, but he grabs my arm and pulls me towards him while angrily demanding that I answer his infuriating question. He totally goes from sweet to an ass one second to the next, and what's worse is I find myself very attracted towards the sweet him.

"How dare you? You truly are a ginormous pain in my backside! Ohhh! How dare you?"

"I demand an answer!" he rants.

"Well, now you are not getting one! Get out or I'll call the garda!"

"I'd like to see you try," he snarls. He pushes me against the back door and kisses me demandingly again.

"Does he kiss you like that?" he demands.

Once I get my breath back, I giggle and answer, "No, just nibbles at my hand!"

He kisses me again, and my door opens in and we fall into the house, on to the floor. "Ouch!"

Patrick rolls over on top of me and continues to kiss me, and now things are getting out of control as his kisses are passionate and wild. Finally, we stop, both breathing hard and staring into each other's eyes. Neither of us seems capable of speaking. He rolls off me, stands, and helps me up. He whispers, "I think I had better leave or I won't be going 'til morn."

I can only nod my head because I'm thinking the same thing, and I hardly know this devilish man. At first, I think it must be hormonal, my desire for him, but that is ridiculous as I'm not a teenager by a long shot. I may still be a virgin at twenty-nine, but I'm well-read on this intimacy topic. My body and I are ready to be loved! With Patrick it feels like my life is on a roller coaster—slow and pokey then, in a second, a speed demon. I really need to think about everything.

SIX

I text Rose and Bevin to see if we could meet somewhere or if they could come to the cottage for dinner one night. I want to take them on a girls' day trip to Dublin to get our hair done, get mani/pedis, and especially beg them to help me find a dress for some upcoming events, like the town music festival and dance. I'm a real mess when it comes to style, but Rose administrates a large, well-known hotel and seldom takes a day off—she's always well dressed. Bevin works for the O'Rileys in their kitchen and has a magical touch with bread and pastries. She really should have her own business. Both girls are a delight, with charming smiles and bubbly laughs; red-haired beauties who are shy around men.

We finally meet for an early dinner in the center, and they tell me they can both get Friday off, which is perfect as Saturday is the festival followed by the outdoor dance. We take the train in the morning and head to our spa time. Rose and Bevin have their hair cut and styled with some highlights, and they are practically glowing from the attention. Brian, the owner of the salon/spa, comments on my hair, as he's never seen anything like it. He says that I have what looks like a five-centimeter strip of golden blonde hair around the top of my head while the rest of my hair is reddish blonde. He dubs me "My Queen" and everyone laughs. I say just a trim and a deep conditioner that makes my hair shine.

We're on to dresses, and the three of us buy a couple of day dresses then something special for the evening. Rose gets a lovely deep-pink maxi dress, and Bevin has to be talked into a short deep-green dress with multiple layers that will swirl around her enticingly as she dances. I find a beautiful floral embroidery mesh over-lay maxi dress in lavender that calls to me, which Rose insists is perfect. I buy us hats to wear for the afternoon musical festival as that, too, will be outside.

Both Rose and Bevin have to work on Saturday morning but have the afternoon and evening off, so we'll go to the dance together. I'm going to the afternoon performances with Ole Annie and a couple of her friends, and they've promised to tell me about the traditional songs and music.

* * *

First up at four is the children's hour; special groups will sing and dance then have a half hour of music for parents and grandparents to dance with their wee ones. It's fascinating to watch how much everyone supports each other and the love of traditional music that is being instilled in the youth.

Next up is the traditional Irish music, and a special feature is the uilleann pipes, fiddles, dulcimer, and Celtic harp among other instruments. The pipes bring a mystical sound of ancient times; hauntingly nostalgic, stimulating my ancestors' blood, I laughingly say.

"Aye lass, I think you are correct in that," Ole Annie says.

SEVEN

There's a break for dinner and then the dance will begin, and from what I hear, it's a lively time with very eclectic music to dance to—from Enya to Adele, modern to oldies. I can't wait, as it sounds like it will be fun. Rose, Bevin, and I meet at their place to eat then change, and as we are finishing getting ready, we can hear the music start up. When we get there, we find a table and get a pitcher of lemonade and a bottle of white wine so we can make our own wine coolers.

Liam is there at the dance and is immediately at our table asking Bevin to dance. She looks a little overwhelmed, but we push her up and they start bouncing to the song. She seems to relax, so Rose and I jump up and start dancing together, and pretty soon it seems like the whole place is vibrating. When the song *Can't Stop The Feeling* starts playing, Antonio is there asking me to dance.

* * *

At the O'Riley Pub, Patrick is at the bar. He told his brothers, Liam and Finn, to go enjoy the dance as he's not really into that stuff and doesn't like to dance. He's just served a couple of Guinness when he gets a text from Finn showing him what he's missing: a video with Tara and Antonio dancing where Antonio keeps putting his hands on Tara's hips.

He yells, "What the feck?" Then he calls to Seamus, his bartender, to handle things and close the place, rips off his apron, and runs out the door.

* * *

Antonio and I just sit down when they start to play music by Enya, something slow and spiritual. Patrick arrives at the table glaring at Antonio, who just smirks at him and says, "Evening, O'Riley—thought you weren't coming."

Patrick ignores him and says, "Lovely evening to ye, Tara, but not as lovely as you."

I stare at him, unable to speak. I'm still a bit angry with him for his stupid comment at the cottage the other night.

"May I have the honor of this dance, my bean álainn?" He extends one hand while his other is on my chair to pull it out for me to stand.

Without thinking, I start to stand and he pulls me towards him and the dance floor. He takes me to the middle then pulls me close, too close, and I try to push back, but he holds me tightly.

His lips are close to my ear and he whispers, "I'm so sorry for what I said the other night. I don't know what came over me, but when we kissed, I think the world stopped and all I could feel was the two of us. I would like to meet your nightly friend if you ever invite me back. I will be a gentleman and not say an unkind word; I promise."

I'm now totally senseless, unable to say anything, and I think we might be moving slightly back and forth—so called dancing—but I'm not sure about that. What is he doing to me? I've been around men all my life—brothers, cousins, and friends—and have had to handle a lot of male dominance at work and with friends. I've never had a problem putting them in their place before, but this man holding me just blows my world apart!

Finally, I find my voice and sigh. "My nightly visitor is an unusually beautiful white deer—a doe—I believe. The first time she showed up it was morning, but now she's coming at night."

"Now, I really feel even smaller than I did before," he comments. "I should know enough to hold my tongue, but my feelings are all over the place when I'm near you, and that's never happened to me before."

"Mr. Patrick O'Riley, I find that hard to believe as you are the most handsome and virile man I have ever met. I find it hard to believe that women aren't falling at your feet. I've seen them at your pub, hanging out at the bar, following you with their eyes, practically drooling to get your attention."

He laughs out loud, and people stop dancing and stare, but he doesn't notice. He bends down and kisses my forehead and says, "I shall repeat myself: I've never felt like I do now. You may have seen those women, but I can't say that I have—well, I see them as customers, that's all. As a good bartender, I smile and make small talk with them, like I do with the men. So, you think I'm handsome, do you?"

Now it's my turn to laugh, and I tell him that he'd better not let the women ever know that he doesn't see them as possible partners.

"What? Everyone in this town—and probably the whole county of Tipperary—knows I'm an established bachelor. Or now perhaps I should say I thought that; I'm not so sure any more," he whispers in my ear.

EIGHT

On Sunday, I'm perplexed. I think it's better to shut myself away; after all, I'm a loner. Or at least I used to be, especially after losing my family in a horrid car crash. But then I think maybe God can give me some insight, so I head to the church of St. John and St. Patrick to ask for guidance. Then I will hurry home and hide for a while.

I see many miserable looking men—suffering from hangovers no doubt—and their complacent wives at the service. The message appears to be about excesses, humility, and service for the greater good. It is calming yet inspiring, plus I learn that there is going to be a special service next Saturday afternoon at the Rock of Cashel—a most unusual event. And it has everyone talking, although I understand that it is basically for the townspeople but all are welcome. I can't wait, as the Rock has drawn me in from the moment I landed in Ireland.

When I leave, I run into Ole Annie and I tell her that I am thrilled about the special service. I ask her if it would be acceptable if I attend and if there is anything I can do to help as I know she is part of the committee that oversees the site. She says, "Aye, sweet child, you must attend, as we'll be divulging the ancient prophesy." Then she says that I should come wearing a lovely gown, purple—if I have one. I have no idea what is going to happen nor that this was such a formal event, but I comment that I'll find one. I want to ask her about the ancient prophesy, but she disappears with a group of people.

While I'm heading towards my bike, I meet Bevin who says that she and Rose would love to help me find a gown as they have to find green ones as well. I ask what it is with the dress code, and she says that it's part of the special service but she doesn't know any more than that. She says that she vaguely remembers her grandparents talking about a prophesy, but she doesn't know what it is. Before I make it to my bike, Patrick is at my side, wishing me a glorious morn and asking me to breakfast.

"To be honest, Patrick, I was going to hide out today, but then I thought God could help me, and all I've done is run into one person after another. Are you sure you want to do this?"

"More than anything, leannán (sweetheart). I would have called you earlier to pick you up but wasn't sure if you'd sleep in today. Perhaps now I can make up for not doing that, if you allow me to."

"Patrick, I was being honest about hiding out as I am so confused about us, and now I'm excited about this coming Saturday and the special service at the Rock. I thought this was a quiet little historical town where I would kick back, relax, and write, but what I've found is a whole different world—and you! I know we need to talk, but . . ."

"Hush, little one, it's alright, ye know. We don't have to rush into anything," laughs Patrick. "And believe me when I say it's all new for me, too. A part of me wants to rush as there's something telling me that ye are the only one for me and I want a forever with ye. Actually, having said that, I think I need a pint or something stronger as I never thought I'd ever think that, let alone say it. For today, let me run you home and then I'll leave you alone, but tell me when I can see you again, please."

"Fine, I appreciate that. Why don't you come to dinner tomorrow night at the cottage? I'm meeting with Bevin and Rose tonight to order our dresses for Saturday."

NINE

ℰarly Saturday morning, and Patrick and his brothers, plus ten other men, are moving benches to the Rock of Cashel, so Antonio is picking me up as I can't very well ride my bike wearing a long gown. Before I leave, I cut some very unique roses that are just blooming out back to leave on the special tomb by the Rock. They are a deep, dark green on the outside, but as they open, they are yellow with green edges. Antonio comments that he's never seen anything like them and wonders if they are heirlooms and unique to Ireland.

When we get near the Rock, Antonio parks and comes with me as I place the roses on the tomb. Once again, a sunbeam hits me as I place the roses on the grave, and I still feel the warmth and vibrations from the stone. I say a special prayer for the ones buried there then turn to head into the chapel where the service is going to be held. I stand still after I've risen and turn slowly as there is a huge animal in front of me. I'm looking at a huge black dog that woofs at me then seems to bow down in front of me. Antonio is as surprised as I am. He tells me it's an Irish Wolfhound. This amazing creature doesn't have a collar, but he is at my side and won't leave me. I scratch his head and tell him what a handsome fellow he is, and then I shrug my shoulders and let him follow me.

I'm planning on sitting in the back, but Ole Annie is waiting for me and leads us to the very front. As I sit down, Paz, my white dove flies in and settles on my shoulder, and I pet her.

The bishop is there and gives everyone a warm welcome, then a children's choir sings. The bishop gives a short prayer and reminds the people of how St. Patrick Christianized the King of Munster at this very site. Then committee in charge of the site comes to the front and says that several special manifestations have occurred, which requires the reading of the Rock's Prophecy. Not many people remember this, so the eldest man of the committee begins to read:

<u>The Irish Kings' Prophecy</u>
    Across the waters
    Deep and wide
    From west to east
    The nymph will glide
    Wings of white will acclaim her
    Fairies will dance their delight
    Twins will attend her
    Moonbeam's light will brighten her night
    A tall dark knight will guard her side
    My legacy shall bloom
    On her throne
    She shall abide

The elders of the town are nodding their heads, while the rest of the people are waiting, hoping that some sort of explanation is coming.

Ole Annie steps up and states, "We received a visitor not long ago; she flew from the west to east to get here." Ole Annie comes over to me and pulls me up, and everyone can see the white dove sitting on my shoulder. It flies up to rest on an outcropping.

Another elderly man steps up and says, "I was cleaning the garden around the Queen's Hideaway before Ms. Tara arrived and it was dry and barren of flowers, but the fairies have worked overtime, and today it is overflowing in blooming flowers and herbs."

Ole Annie continues, "Two unusual kittens have made their home with Tara at the cottage. There are many nights where she also has a unique visitor; an albino doe comes to drink at her stream and keeps her company. Today, you have all seen the appearance of an Irish Wolfhound at her side. Does this creature belong to anyone here?" Ole Annie waits for a couple of minutes, but no one claims the dog.

She continues, "The only thing seemingly missing is the queen's bloom—something exceptional, or so it would appear." Everyone gasps as a strong clap of thunder is heard, yet the sun is shining.

Antonio stands up and says, "Wait one minute and I'll bring that to you as Tara brought some unique roses to put on a grave. They were green on the outside and yellow on the inside." The committee gasps and waits for him to come back in. I turn to Ole Annie to ask her what is going on, but she asks me to be patient.

Antonio comes back in, holding one hand behind his back. The other does not hold any roses. He exclaims, "I cannot say what happened, but the roses were gone and in their place was this." He holds up what appears to be a golden crown that has emeralds embedded around it.

The bishop comes forth and states, "The Kings' Prophecy appears to have been fulfilled and Ireland has her queen. Long live Queen Tara!"

I am in shock; I can't move or speak. I look at Patrick for help, and he's smiling and repeating with the rest of the crowd: "Long live Queen Tara." The bishop places the crown on my head, and it covers the blonde circle in my hair exactly.

I still can't move, but I want to ask them what is happening—is this a joke? But it can't be as everyone is so serious. Patrick comes up, bows, and kisses my hand, followed by Antonio, Finn, and Liam. Bevin and Rose come up, one on either side of me and Ole Annie gestures to them and they curtsy, of all things! She whispers that they are my ladies-in-waiting.

Really! This is too much! I take off running outside and to the special grave, my apparent new guard dog at my side. Paz flies above me until she lands on my shoulder. I kneel down and place my hands on the stone, and I can hear a mystical sound coming from...the uilleann pipes are playing somewhere!

Everyone from the church is surrounding the grave, whispering about the music. Then a communal gasp goes up as a sunbeam lights up the grave and myself, making the crown shine. A child shouts, "Look, a triple rainbow!"

On either side of the grave, a shoot starts to come up from the ground and someone recognizes it as a young branch from a rose bush. I'm feeling dizzy, then strong arms surround me and Patrick helps me to stand.

He says, "It may seem like a fairy tale, but this prophecy has been around for centuries; people have been born and died, always waiting for it to come true, as it will designate our new king or queen. It would appear that your ancestry is in the bloodline of a queen also named Tara from the distant past. It is clear to us here that you are the one who the prophecy mentions. Don't worry too much; it's an honorary title, not a government job!"

"But then this crown is a national heirloom and must be very valuable; it shouldn't belong to me. Where did it come from?"

Antonio says, "It was here on the stone, exactly where you left the roses."

A little girl comes up to me and hands me a bouquet of wild flowers, and I bend down to take them and give her a kiss on her cheek while thanking her. She runs back laughing. "Mam, the Queen kissed me!"

I'm feeling dizzy again! I just can't wrap my head around this! I need to hide away or run away, something! It comes to me again, how much I've changed, but I'm not sure that I'm comfortable with these changes.

The people shout, "To the park to welcome our queen!" The people line up on either side of the path, the bishop leads the way, Patrick offers me his arm, and we walk back to the park. Paz is flying overhead, the wolfhound is in front of me, Bevin and Rose are behind me, while the committee members follow; it's quite the parade. When we reach the park, Antonio brings out a very impressive high-back chair and sets in near the fountain in the shade.

I whisper to Patrick, "This is a joke, right? What am I supposed to do now?"

He whispers back, "It's no joke, but I think you should ask Ole Annie as I have no idea what's to come—although it looks like you are supposed to sit here and receive homage from your subjects. Allow me to be the first. He kneels then says in a quiet voice, "Whatever your heart desires, allow me to give it to you. I am at your eternal service, my beautiful queen."

"My dear Patrick, what I would love to do right now is smack you, you cheeky cad!"

TEN

I sit there until I am numb as I greet everyone in town, which seems like thousands today. I kiss babies and toddlers and have my hand kissed, over and over. Patrick goes back to his pub as it is sure to be filled to the rafters with townspeople. Finally, Antonio comes and rescues me and takes me to his restaurant, along with Bevin and Rose. Ole Annie finds us and says that I have a meeting with the committee and town officers on Monday, so it seems things are just starting, not winding down. I receive a frantic call from Patrick, asking where I am. There's a long silence when I tell him and finally he snaps out, "Okay, bye."

Now, I'm a bit upset with his attitude, but I suppose it's typically a male thing. We spend another relaxing half hour then I thank Antonio and head out. Bevin and Rose don't live far, so we're walking. I say that I'm going to go to the pub and they just nod; they're not going to tell me it's a bad idea, even though I'm still wearing the crown—cripe, I forgot I had it!

The O'Riley Pub is rocking; music is playing, people are singing and seems like everyone is quite happy indeed. I sneak a peek through the window of the door, and Finn sees me and comes out. I ask him for Patrick, and he tells me that he's in his office banging stuff around. I beg him to sneak me through, which won't be easy as my dog won't leave my side. He takes me around to the back door and through the kitchen and shows me which is the office door. He bangs on it then leaves. Patrick shouts, "I said I didn't want to see anyone! Go away!"

I open the door and question, "Not even the person you are supposedly courting?"

My dog pushes through and goes over to Patrick and looks up at him until he gets his ears rubbed, then he plops down. Patrick just stares at me then starts in. "Ye didn't come through the pub looking like that, did ye?"

"What's wrong with the way I look?"

"You're wearing the feckin' crown, you know?" he snaps.

"Might I inquire as to your unique mood? Did something bad happen?"

"Yes, you were with Antonio! There, is that what you wanted to know?" he shoots back.

"Jealousy does not become you, Mr. O'Riley. I thought you understood that men and women can be just friends." I step up to him and punch him in the chest with my finger.

He just stares at me for a while then finally says, "I apologize. I'm just not good at the dating game."

"Well, to me it's not a game and it's not an affair, so I'm thinking that we are forming a relationship; something serious as I consider myself too old to be playing 'games' with the opposite sex."

"Oh, thank the Lord!" Patrick declares. "I was thinking or hoping or wishing, that I knew what you thought. I'm not an expert at this; never done it before, ye know."

"I guess we'll learn how to do things together then as I'm no expert myself—I've been a bit of a loner after losing my family. I was hoping I might persuade you to give us a ride back to the cottage, if you're not too busy and can take the time."

"For you, my queen, I have all the time you need, and if I'm busy, I'll make time—you'll always come first!" Patrick is on a roll.

On the way home, Patrick says that Saturdays are always a busy night but this night is especially busy due to the prophecy coming true. I mention that we really need to talk about that and ask why no one ever mentioned it to me.

"Personally," Patrick admits, "I had completely forgotten about it. It's not like it's mentioned every day. Probably a lot of the younger people didn't even know that it existed. I'm thinking that maybe my maimeó might have told us the story long ago, but it's only a vague memory. "

ELEVEN

When we reach the cottage, Patrick hands me a huge dog bed, collar, and leash and asks me to take them as he has a bag of dog food—all things he thought of and I didn't. I swirl around, drop everything, and hug him, saying he's such a thoughtful, loving man. He hugs me back and goes in for the kiss, and it's a lovely one that gets interrupted by a whine and a wet nose.

"I believe someone is hungry."

I pick up the things and head to the door. With my hands full, I just say, "Please open, my darling door!" It swings open and Patrick just stares at me and asks, "What just happened?"

"Oh, didn't I mention that one day I was out back and I forgot the stone so I politely asked the door to open and it did? Well, that's something I suppose I should tell Ole Annie.

"Do you know if there's a safe in the cottage? I need to store this crown somewhere secure." Strange as it may be, Truffle jumps up on the mantel over the fire-place, meows, then puts his paw on an iron flower decoration. Patrick goes over and looks at it then tries to turn it, but it doesn't move. Then he pushes it, and there's a scraping sound and a stone on the outside of the fireplace moves and we see a hollow space. Patrick turns on the flashlight app on his phone, and we find a dark cloth inside. He pulls it out, and I unfold it; inside is a beautiful necklace and a ring that's gold with emeralds and very, very old! We stare at them astounded.

"Well, I guess that would be a good place to keep the crown!" I say.

"So, it would appear. These two definitely are the 'twins that attend you' in the prophesy."

"Patrick, can we sit and talk for a bit? Would you like a cup of tea?"

"Yes, thank you; I'd enjoy both."

Patrick starts a fire as I make the tea, then we sit in front of it and I start with the easier of the questions. "I would love your suggestions on names for my new friend here. It may be that he is 'my tall, dark knight,' or perhaps that's you! Anyways, this lovely dog needs a name."

"Let's see...no, no idea. Sir something as the prophecy said he'd be a knight. Oh, what about Dylan? It means faithful and loyal."

"I love it. What do you think, Sir Dylan?" I get a woof in reply. "Now for the problem or dilemma I find myself in; I don't think it's right for an American to be the 'Irish Queen.' First of all, did you know about today and what was going to happen?"

"No, though honestly, I was not totally shocked as I've heard that there have been others who Ole Annie have let stay here but only for a couple of days as there was 'nothing special about them after all,' or so she said. 'Just tricksters.' I vaguely remembered the prophecy, which is the same, I think, for most people because it's centuries old and, like most old things, mostly forgotten. I was surprised to see ye dressed up in purple, the color of royalty, and then Bevin and Rose in green; quite the sight the three of ye!"

"Aye Patrick, I don't know what to do, but I don't feel good about this. I'm so tired! Everything that happened and then the bishop declaring me Queen of Ireland—I think he shouldn't have said that. It can lead to a lot of problems for everyone, in particular, the town. Truthfully, not once in my life have I ever dreamed of being a princess, let alone a queen. I believe royalty is born into it, like Kate and William's children, and not due to a prophecy. Maybe this town is happy about it, but I doubt the county will be, much less the country. I may have to leave sooner than expected."

"You can't leave now!" Patrick begs. "We're just starting our courting, and I don't want to lose ye; you're all I can think about. Please say you won't run away!"

"I can't do that to Ole Annie; I owe her so much. But I wish she had talked to me about this, not just thrust me into this situation. Plus I wouldn't do that to you. I can hardly think as it is." I rest my head on Patrick's shoulder and quickly fall asleep.

TWELVE

The next thing I know, there's a pounding on the door, and I wake up on top of my bed still dressed in my gown. Patrick's arm is around me, and he's sleeping beside me. Oh, boy, this isn't good!

I make it to the door with Sir Dylan at my side and find Antonio and Finn. They come in and see Patrick sitting up on the bed, yawning.

I am startled but manage, "It's not what it looks like! We didn't . . ."

The two of them start laughing, and Patrick throws a pillow at them, which Dylan picks up and takes back to him. Finn can finally say, "It's obvious that the two of you spent the night together, so don't even try to deny it." He laughs his head off.

"Of course, being completely dressed in yesterday's clothes does look a mite confusing, right, Finn?" pipes up Antonio.

"Well, I'm glad to see our disheveled state makes you laugh. Is there a reason that the two of ye are here so early?" Patrick isn't any too pleased about the visit.

"Actually, we figured that you'd want to put in an appearance at church today—it being Sunday and all. Not much time to get ready, but I managed to bring you a different shirt to be on the safe side."

"I suppose that would be the correct thing to do. I may not be on board with this whole queen thing, but I am not a snob and don't want people to think that I'm ignoring them. I am just so confused!"

Finn and Antonio take off, and we follow shortly behind—once I change my clothes and Patrick puts on the shirt that Finn brought.

When we reach the church, the bishop is waiting for us and leads us to the front. So much for going unnoticed. I even hear whispers of, "She's not wearing her crown." Ole Annie comes over and places a crown of wildflowers on my head and gives me a pat on my shoulder. I shall pray for guidance on what I should do; only God knows what is going on. Paz flies in and alights on my shoulder.

When the service ends, the bishop escorts me to the doors and I end up greeting everyone again as they leave! This is too much! I feel like running away! Patrick must feel something as he places his hand on my lower back, and somehow that infuses me with stillness. Finally, Ole Annie is next, and I give her a kiss on the cheek and whisper, "You have a lot of explaining to do!" She just smiles and says, "See you tomorrow at the Halla an Bhaile at ten."

I have to ask Patrick what she said, and he replies that that is the Town Hall.

THIRTEEN

onday morning, I ride my bike to the Town Hall. Last night, I compiled a list of questions for the committee, town elders, or whoever is at this meeting today, as well as reasons why I can't possibly be the Queen of Ireland.

Imagine my surprise that when upon arriving, I am greeted as Queen Tara and led to sit in front of a large group of people. The bishop stands and proceeds to say that he has contacted the Archbishop of the Republic of Ireland, and they are preparing a further symbolic test for me in the spring in County Meath. For the County of Tipperary, I have been acknowledged as the new and rightful queen, but I will have no official obligations. In the spring, a formal delegation will accompany me to a special site for the day, and with that, my future will be decided.

I'm not sure what they are talking about, but I truly am getting agitated about 'my future being decided' by someone other than myself. I am about to say so but find that I cannot speak, literally—*What the feck?*

As I stand, everyone does the same, and they bow! I am beyond confused and really ticked off, but Patrick comes up to me, kneels then offers his arm, and we go back to his pub. When we reach it, he offers me an Irish coffee and says, "Now, lass, that wasn't so bad was it?"

I am ready to pull my hair out and tell him that for some inexplicable reason, I lost my power of speech—literally lost it—when all I really wanted to do was tell them that I am not the Queen of Ireland, and never will be and that whatever they have planned for me is unnecessary.

Patrick goes on to tell me that he has an idea that we'll be visiting the Hill of Tara and the Stone of Destiny at the spring solstice and there is nothing to worry about. He tells me I can Google it and that it is an ancient site that the Irish are very proud of and respect.

* * *

For a couple of months, things are almost back to normal, with only a few special invitations to visit schools and the hospital as Queen Tara. I've been able to write and have finished a new book and sent it off to my publisher. Patrick and I are exclusive and enjoying each other's companying. Rose, Bevin, and I have had another girls' weekend in Dublin, and I've almost forgotten about the spring solstice and have halfway forgotten about being queen.

I am enjoying myself at the O'Riley Pub so much that time gets away from me, and when I finally look out a window, I see that it is getting dark. I jump up and hurriedly say my goodbyes as Sir Dylan and I start for home. We are nearing my cottage when some little animal runs across the road in front of me, and when I jerk the bike to the right, I hit a pothole and lose control. I'm flying over the handlebars and hit something hard and then blackness over takes me.

FOURTEEN

 come to but have no idea where I am, nor the time, as the bed I'm in is so different from mine at the cottage and the room is dark. I feel Sir Dylan's head next to my arm, and he whines, then woofs.

A door opens, and an elderly woman comes in, saying, "Don't be scared, little one, my name is Megan. My son Quinn was coming back from Cashel last night and said he saw ye fall off your bike, so he stopped to help but ye were knocked out. He's a simple boy and didn't know what to do, so he brought ye back home, along with yer dog—and a fine guard he is. How are ye feeling?"

"My head is pounding and I think my right wrist is sprained but nothing seems to be broken. Thank you so much for taking care of me. Where am I?"

"My son and I live on the outskirts of Tipperary," explains Megan. "It's a wee bit of a ways from where he found ye but not too far. What's yer name, little one?"

"Oh, I . . . I'm not sure."

"Well now, it doesn't matter. Ye're not wearing a wedding ring, so it looks like ye're not married. Hopefully someone will be looking for ye though. When Quinn has time, he can go back to Cashel to ask if anyone is missing. Now, best ye rest. I'll wrap up your wrist so it doesn't move too much. Here's some broth and bread to fill yer stomach." It seems like I just finish the broth before I fall asleep.

* * *

Back at Cashel the following day, Patrick calls me but it goes to voicemail. He asks Bevin and his brothers if I said what I was going to do, but no one has any idea. He decides to go to my house, but it looks like no one is there as my bike is gone. As he goes up to the door, it opens and the kittens are making quite the fuss, which is distracting as I always have food out for them. He feeds them and looks around, but nothing else seems to be out of place.

Suddenly, Paz flies inside and lands on his shoulder, pecks his ear, then flies out the door. Patrick grabs his ear but follows Paz outside. The dove flies down the road, maybe twenty meters, then lands on the side near a ditch. Patrick is curious, so he runs down to see and finds my bike with my bag still in the basket. My cell phone is in the bag. He notices a rock near my bike with blood on it, and he immediately calls his brothers and the garda.

Patrick is beside himself, shouting at the garda, calling the hospital, Ole Annie, even Antonio, but no one has seen me. Antonio comes flying down the road and finally convinces Patrick to go back to my cottage and wait as it seems like that is where I would probably reappear. He wants all the taxi drivers questioned and people at the railroad as he wonders if I left the country. He's totally lost it and forgetting there was blood at the scene. Ole Annie tries to convince him that I probably went somewhere for help.

The following day, in Tipperary, I'm stronger now and my head hurts less, but I'm still too dizzy to walk around. Megan comes in and says I need to rest until my head is better as it's quite a big bump that I have. I wish I could remember more, but at least I have my dog. She says that Quinn is out in the fields with his sheep and won't be back for a couple of days. She gives me an old dress of hers and tells me to give her my clothes and she'll wash them. She brings me soap and water to bathe myself but tells me not to touch my head as she bandaged the cut and it needs to heal.

Two more days go by, then Quinn returns. He's a gentle young man, slow to speak and act but loving to my dog. He and his mother raise a large flock of sheep, card and spin the wool, and make beautiful sweaters which they sell. They also have a huge garden, several hens, a few goats, and a couple of beef animals. They are very proud, independent Irish. Their home is rustic but comfortable. They don't have a television, let alone a computer. They have a radio, but it's broken right now.

I feel safe and relaxed here, even though I can't remember who I am or what I do here in Ireland. Megan says that my accent is a bit Irish but a bit strange. Once I'm able to get around, I ask her to let me help her with the chores. Quinn comes and goes, taking care of his sheep. It's been ten days, and I'm starting to wonder who I am. Megan tries to teach me how to knit, but all I can manage is the ribbing.

Tomorrow, Quinn will take me back to Cashel and, if he remembers, near to where he found me to see if something feels like it's home.

The next day, when we get near to where he thinks I had my accident, we see a garda car and another one next to a small cottage, so we stop and get out. Patrick is there and screams, "Tara!" as he runs to grab me up, but the garda seize hold of Quinn, who becomes upset and confused.

"Let him go! Please, he's done nothing but help me!" I go up to Quinn and hold his hand. "This man found me in the ditch and took me to his mother's to heal. He's a very good man, aren't you, Quinn?"

Quinn can barely stutter an aye to that.

Patrick comes up and puts his arm around me and I pull away quickly, saying, "Who are you? Do you know me?"

Patrick is stunned. "You're Tara Connors, my love, my girlfriend. Don't ye remember me?"

I turn to the garda and ask them if they know me, and one of them says, "Aye, you are Queen Tara, recently crowned queen of Ireland, and you live here at the Queen's Hideaway."

"What?"

Quinn looks as confused as I am, but he takes off his cap and bows to me.

"Quinn, Quinn, it's okay, it's still me." I lay a reassuring hand on his arm.

The other garda suggests we all go into the cottage and have a cuppa tea. Patrick makes it, and I sit next to Quinn, who is very shy, but the two kittens come over to him and get in his lap, which makes him smile. Sir Dylan sits between Quinn and myself. Patrick calls his brothers to report my return, and they call the others.

We all sit down, and Quinn slowly retells them how he saw my accident and took me home. The garda want to know why it took so long for him to return this way. I tell them that he has sheep to take care of and his mother took care of me and that they are both great people. The garda say that they are proud to meet Quinn and he and his mother will be honored for helping the Queen. Quinn looks confused, and I try to comfort him and tell him that I'm still me but now I have a name, which makes him smile.

Patrick keeps looking at me sadly. I can tell he's hurt that I don't remember him, but, jeez, I still don't remember my own name! Quinn says that he needs to get back to his mother, so I give him a hug, thank him, and tell him I would like to visit them in a few days. He says that's fine and goodbye.

The garda are ready to leave when there is an influx of people streaming into the cottage. Patrick says he thinks it would be a good idea for me to go to hospital to be checked out. I tell him that it is not necessary, that I feel fine, I just seem to have some kind of amnesia. He wants to know if I remember anything about the cottage. All I can tell him is that it feels like home. I ask him the name of the kittens and my dog. He also tells me that there is a white dove that I call Paz around most of the time. He says that at least I had Sir Dylan with me to keep me safe. I thank him for telling me the names of my animal friends and ask him if he can ask all the people to give me a few days to recover here on my own.

He doesn't think I should be alone but reluctantly agrees. He tells me that my cell phone is on the table and that he charged it and that he's number one on my speed dial if I need anything. I tell him that he'll be the first I'll call if I need something, but right now, I need to relax and think.

FIFTEEN

I put on some Celtic music, make more tea, and head out back where I see a beautiful garden. I'm sitting there alone but not alone at all as there's my sweetheart of a dog at my feet, two frisky kittens, and a white dove that Patrick called Paz. I feel something deep within me, something I can't put words to, but it makes me feel loved. Now, I see a white deer coming out of the woods. She strolls up to the brook and drinks, then she comes over and nuzzles my hand. She's magical, I can feel it. Suddenly, it sounds like uilleann pipes are playing an eerie, ancient tune—not only that but my flowers are swaying to the tune. There are sparkling lights all around me; they are so comforting that I lay down for a bit. My head feels light and I feel like I'm floating on a rainbow. Some time later, I wake up as Sir Dylan is licking my face and the kittens are batting my arms. I must have dosed off. I pick up my cup and head into the cottage to feed my friends and go to bed. I'm dosing off, but the little lights are still flying around my room, lulling me to sleep.

In the morning I grab my phone and text Patrick—*My sweet Patrick, tis a lovely morn. When will I see you, my love? Soon, I hope!*

In less than fifteen minutes, Patrick is at the door. My magical doors that now seem to open automatically, not only for me but for Patrick as well, swing open. He just stands there in the doorway, looking at me, then tentatively says, "Tara?"

"Yes, my handsome man, who else?"

He's wrapping me in his arms in a second and kissing me the next. I feel truly blessed: this country, these people, this man!

"Oh, Patrick, you'll never believe what happened yesterday afternoon." I proceed to tell him about all my 'little friends' and then the colorful lights, that truly must be fairies, and the mystical music, as well as falling asleep outside. We're still standing there holding each other.

"Well, mo bhanrion (my queen)," sighs Patrick. "So many thoughts ran through my head when you went missing. I came here and the door opened for me then and the kittens were starving and I knew something was wrong. It was Paz that showed me where you went off the road and that you were hurt, and it was all I could do to call me brothers. I even accepted Antonio's help, and Ole Annie was beside herself. There have been people praying night and day for your safe return."

I've fed my four-legged friends, but I can't remember when I last ate, so it's myself who's starving now.

"Let's go to the pub and you're going to have a town full of people to say hello to, so it will be a long day,"

Patrick comments. He calls his brothers to let them know that we'll be there shortly for breakfast and to invite Ole Annie, Antonio, and Rose if she can get away from the hotel.

I think if Patrick could get away with it, he'd be holding me on his lap. It hits me how close we've become; he really is a special man. He's at my side the whole time we're at the pub, making sure I don't get too tired but do get to thank everyone for their prayers.

Finally, it's late afternoon and Patrick decides it's time to take me home. Sir Dylan is happy to be back at the cottage, and he and Truffle and Caramel head out to the garden to lay in the sun. Patrick just stands here, holding me and kisses my neck. He asks if he can do anything for me. "Would I like a cuppa tea?"

"No, my love, what I want is you. You'll be my first."

We forget about dinner and make love all night long. I've never known what love for a man was before but we seem to be made perfectly, one for the other—ying for yang, Romeo and Juliet without the sad parts, Burton and Taylor, and all the other great love stories throughout history.

SIXTEEN

I'm still writing, but I inform my publisher that I'm planning on living in Ireland permanently. I tell her that I'm embarking on a new kind of book: a journal of a new queen. She had heard about something unusual happening but didn't realize that it was me who the article was referring to and now she's all for it.

The months go by, and soon it's time for the trip to Meath County. It appears that there will be delegations from each county in the country and even Northern Ireland has indicated interest.

Ole Annie asks me to wear my long purple gown and to bring the crown and jewels that we found. On the day that we head to Meath, Patrick comes to pick me up as we're all going on the train and then buses will take us to the Hill of Tara. When we go to get in Patrick's car, I find two large bouquets of flowers from my garden, it seems, and I thank Patrick, but he says that it wasn't him and they weren't there before. "Oh well, the fairies are working overtime," I laugh. There is also a ceremonial athame (dagger) on the seat, which I hand to Patrick to carry for me.

There seems to be hundreds of people waiting at the site, and when our bus arrives, the Archbishop of Ireland greets me and tells me that they have several things to ask me—the first being if I have ever been to visit this site before today. I tell him that I googled it and read up on its history but have never visited it. He says that the governing committee, which includes the president and prime minister of the country want to politely ask me if I mind taking this this test blindfolded. Patrick immediately says that that is not necessary and could lead to me falling. I state that I have every faith in Patrick and his catching me if I start to fall.

Paz alights on my shoulder, and I am surprised but pleased, and of course, Sir Dylan has accompanied us, as well. Paz flies over to a fence, and I ask what is there. A national historian says that that is the site of the Well of the White Cow. I say that apparently I need to carry some of its water with me, and I walk over and collect some in an old flask that I find there. I return to the archbishop, and he blindfolds me, then Patrick kisses me gently and says, "No matter what happens, we have each other forever and always." I am turned around several times then asked to start whenever I wish. I pat Sir Dylan on the head and feel Paz on my shoulder, and then I begin my walk. I do not go very far when I feel a force that stops me. It turns me to my right, and I walk maybe three meters and stop again. I ask if there is something of importance here and the historian steps up and states that I am standing at the Mound of Hostages. I thank her and ask Patrick to hand me a bouquet of our flowers, which he does, and then I throw them up into the air and I expect they settle on the mound. I tell Patrick that I need the athame, and he asks for what. "All I can say is that some invisible force is telling me what to do." He gently hands me the knife, and I hear gasps as I cut my left palm then turn it so my blood drips down onto the mound. I ask for a little of the water to pour over my hand, then I kneel.

"Dear ancient gods, goddesses, and our God, I wish to thank all the fallen warriors for their bravery and sacrifice. I know without a doubt that their gods, goddesses and our God bless them for their sacrifice. May you rest in peace. Amen." I hear more gasps and some disgruntled mumbling, but I stand and begin walking again.

I walk for a ways and when I stop I say, "Patrick please take my hand. We need to give thanks: To the north for the air." We turn. "To the east for fire, to the south for water, and to the west for earth."

Next, I drop Patrick's hand and turn around with my hands out in front of me and slowly walk forward until my hands meet with stone. I ask Patrick for the other flowers. Keeping an elbow on the stone and using the other hand, I place them around the base of the stone, then the water, and once again, I ask for the athame. Patrick is more hesitant but hands it to me. This time I place the blade over my heart and make five small pricks in the shape of a cross, then I take some of my blood on my left hand and touch the stone.

I kneel and feel the stone start to warm, and the warmth travels up my arms, and I embrace it. The archbishop uncovers my eyes, and I stare at the stone and smile. The sun breaks through the clouds, and the stone is bathed in strong sunbeams. It is very big and impressive, more so than one can learn off the internet. I tilt my head as I swear I can hear a harp, then the uilleann pipes, then a drum and a flute. The crowd has gone silent listening to the mystical song. When the song dies out, the stone seems to send up a cry of joy. I can't figure out how that can happen, but then so many things have happened to me here in the Emerald Isle that strange has become acceptable and not at all scary.

I look over my shoulder and see tears on Patrick's cheeks. I offer him my hand again and ask him if he heard the music.

Patrick says, "Aye, it's the *Song for Ireland,* a very beloved song in all of the country."

The historian comes up and offers us a cup of something, which I expect I must drink some of, so I do. Then I hand it to Patrick, and he takes a drink and gives it back to the historian, saying, "Fine Irish ale."

I ask him if he feels the warmth from the stone, so we place our hands together on the stone, and he says that it does feel warm and then we feel a vibration from it. We turn to each other and kiss. The archbishop, president, and prime minister come up to us. The archbishop turns to take the pillow, on which the crown has been placed, raises it high and states solemnly, "The Lord our Father, our ancient kings and the Stone of Destiny have decreed—Queen Tara the II—long may you reign, long live the Queen of Ireland!" Before his hands touch the crown, there is a roll of thunder and a crack of lightning, then a strong ray of sunlight hits the purple cushion and the crown shines like newly polished gold and the emeralds sparkle. He places the crown on my head. Then the president steps forward and places the necklace around my neck. The prime minister hands Patrick the ring, which he places on my right hand. Ole Annie, Rose, and Bevin are openly crying and then kneeling, but now I see that the archbishop, the president and the prime minister and all in the crowd have also knelt. Patrick shouts, "Long live the Queen!" The crowd erupts with cheers. I feel like I'm in another dimension, in a dream world that I cannot awaken from!

Well, I fondly remember my time spent in the quietude with Megan and Quinn, but something moves inside me and I straighten my spine and smile. I am ready for this!

Before I can move, once again an invisible force turns me back to the stone, and again, I place my hands on it. It feels like I'm being pulled around it until I see a line going into the ground. I kneel and clear a small area and feel something hard. I clear the dirt and find something silver, and it rises into my hand. I pull out a sword! The force turns me to Patrick, and I tell him to kneel (in an ancient tongue) then touch the sword to his shoulders and knight him, then I hand him the sword. I feel dizzy, and Patrick comes and wraps an arm around me to steady me, and the crowd goes wild with cheering and clapping. Once again, there is music from celestial drums and flutes!

As everyone stands, the historian is whispering to the archbishop, who nods, smiles, then says, "As the legend implies, with the drinking of the ale and the touching of the Stone of Destiny, the two of you are now married. It would also suffice to say that our new queen has knighted you Sir Patrick."

Patrick and I look at each other; both of us are astonished. I feel I should have read the legends more carefully. Patrick is grinning as he says, "That was a very short ceremony; I like it, my wife and my queen!"

I briefly consider knocking him on his arse but decide it wouldn't look dignified to the crowd, so I whisper to him instead, "Wait until we are alone, and you'll see, Sir Patrick!"

"I can't wait for our wedding night, my love, my queen!" Patrick smiles.

The historian comes up and whispers to the two of us, "The marriage part is symbolic, of course, your highness."

SEVENTEEN

All I want is to head home and go to my little cottage for a cuppa, to see my garden, and my sweet animals! I am so not into pomp and aristocracy. I cannot even conceive what will be expected of me, and I cringe.

The prime minister comes up and says that everyone is extremely pleased to have an Irish queen again, but that I shouldn't worry about my obligations as they, in the government, have much to discuss about this topic and it will take time. But I might want to hide out for a while to avoid all the reporters and the like, although they will be expecting some comments and interviews, and I should think about preparing for that. He assures me that he will be preparing an official announcement in the next few days.

When we come down from the hill, I am introduced to all the heads of the counties and many other VIPs. Finally, we are allowed to get on our bus to return to the train and start our trip home.

During the train ride, I'm questioned about my actions by my friends.

I mention that Paz was what led me to the well, but I *felt* a need for water and there just happened to be an old flask next to the well. Then, I say, as I was walking, some *invisible force* led me to what I was told was the Mound of Hostages. There, I *felt* a need to honor the dead and that was through the flowers, water, and my blood. The athame had appeared in Patrick's car, and it seemed right to bring it along. The cutting of my palm—I *felt* like a ghost was doing it then holding my hand over the mound. When that was done, I sensed the invisible force leading me up a walkway and finally up a hill. There was a whisper in my ear: *Take Patrick's hand and salute the four directions and the elements.* When that was done, *the force* turned me and gently pulled me to the stone where I touched its rounded face and therefore could place flowers around its base. Once again, I sensed the need for the athame and a *ghostly hand* pricked my chest, which surprised me, but then it placed my hand over the knife then on the stone. When I saw the stone, it brought happiness to me and it was warm to the touch. I asked Patrick to touch it as well, and he felt it and its vibration. I have no idea about the music, but it was beautiful. After I was crowned, *the force* once again returned me to the stone and led me to the sword and then spoke through me when I knighted Patrick and gave him the sword. When the spirit left me, I felt dizzy.

After telling my story, I am both mentally and physically drained. When we finally reach Cashel, Patrick puts me into his car and drives me home. When we get out of the car, my Irish Wolfhound/knight hackles rise as he stands in front of my door. The door is shut tight and it's not like just anyone can get in, but we know something is disturbing Sir Dylan.

Patrick tells the door to open, and he tells me to stay back, but I'm not going to let him get hurt. Sir Dylan pushes by us and goes to stand next to the table, where I see a light shimmering—purples and greens streaking through it. Truffle and Caramel are laying on the table, purring, and it looks like something is petting them. Dylan sits down and now it looks like something is scratching him behind his ears.

I ask Patrick if he sees what I see, and he says, "Aye." The next thing I see is a cloth bag landing on the table and a piece of parchment floating down. The ghost or spirit or whatever this is floats towards me, but it doesn't instill fear as I feel a warmth surround me, then it vanishes.

"Holy Mother Mary! That was something! It wasn't scary, which I'm sure it probably should have been; it felt comforting." Patrick goes and picks up the note and comments that it is written in an ancient language; something like Goidelic or primitive Irish, he's not sure, but a historian would probably know of someone who might be able to translate it. I go over, and he passes the note to me, and it spreads warmth up my arm, and I tell him that whatever is written, it's affectionate and caring.

Next, Patrick hands me the bag, but I ask him to open it, so he turns it out onto the table. Rings, necklaces, a tiara, and brooches fall out of the bag; all of them look very, very old. There are rings of both silver and gold, some with gemstones. There is a golden torc necklace and a lunula, necklace also in gold. There is a silver torc bracelet and a beautiful Celtic cross with jewels encrusted in it as well as a Tara brooch. I wish we could read the note, perhaps it would tell us what we are supposed to do with the jewels. Patrick says that for now, we'll have to see how much of it will fit into the secret hidey-hole with the crown. Surprisingly, the sword appears to have a place to hang above the fireplace.

We finally make it to bed, and our symbolic wedding night is one to remember. I wonder what kind of real wedding I will be allowed to have, as I am now carrying around the title of queen. Perhaps we should plan a really quick one before the government can intervene.

Oh right, how silly—my black-haired lover hasn't proposed and I'm beginning to wonder if he will. What have I done?

EIGHTEEN

The next morning, I sneak out of bed, grab my robe, make myself a cuppa, and head for the back garden with Sir Dylan, Caramel, and Truffle. I sit on the stone wall and contemplate my situation, until finally I say out loud, "What am I to do with Patrick?"

At that moment, Patrick clears his throat, comes over, wearing just his jeans, and kisses me. Then he questions, "What would you like to do with me, mo grá?"

"What does that mean?"

"It means my love and can also mean my wife," Patrick says.

"But legally we're not married, according to the historian. I was just wondering what we are."

"Tara, my love, I knew from the first time I met you that you are special. I couldn't stop thinking about you and wanting to be near you. I love you with all my Irish heart and soul," Patrick states. Then he gets down on one knee and continues, "I was going to ask you at the Hill of Tara but the huge number of strangers there was too great. But now, here—will you do me the honor of becoming my wife?"

"Yes, Patrick! Yes, a thousand times yes. I love you so much."

He hands me a beautiful gold ring with an emerald heart and a series of diamonds around the top of the heart, then gently places it on my ring finger.

"This is a Claddagh ring," he says, "and with the heart pointing towards you, it means you are engaged and I will turn it on our wedding so it will mean that you are married. It's a family heirloom, and I've been saving it for you, the woman who has filled my heart, my soul, and my life with love."

We decide to spend a wee bit longer in bed to celebrate our engagement. Afterwards, we talk about getting married, and we both want to do it quickly but are concerned about being allowed to do it quietly due to the situation I find myself in. I'm also worried about Patrick having his life turned upside down and if he's willing or able to do what will be expected of us as a royal couple. I'm not sure that I'm willing to become a public figure either. Life as I knew it no longer exists! I am ready to embrace change, but I'm not really sure what all these changes will require of me.

Patrick suggests that we have a family dinner to announce our engagement. He says that Antonio has a private dining room at his restaurant, and he'll invite Ole Annie as well.

During the day, I seem to float around the cottage, singing and petting my friends. Just before Patrick arrives to pick me up, I receive a phone call from the prime minister's office asking me to come to Dublin on Friday to discuss my future here in Ireland. I agree but say that I'll be bringing a few friends with me as well.

* * *

The dinner starts off with toasts to the new queen and the newly knighted Patrick. Patrick and I stand up, and he tells everyone that he asked me to marry him and I said yes, and I show them the ring. We mention that we would like to be married as quickly and as quietly as possible, here in Cashel. I then tell them that I have to be in Dublin on Friday to go to Parliament to learn what the government has decided, and I would love for some of them to accompany me.

Ole Annie says she understands my plight and will speak with the bishop the following day. She asks if we have thought of where we want to be married. Patrick says, "I think Tara would prefer the Rock as it seems to have a special hold on her."

"I would, but I'm not sure how the bishop will feel about that."

Finn says, "We could have a reception after at the pub, if you'd like."

Antonio adds, "I'll help with the food as well, and I'm sure with Liam, Finn, and Bevin we can come up with something grand, although I've no idea about a wedding cake."

"I think a traditional cake is called for and would be appreciated by the ancestors, as they seem to have a say in all these goings on."

NINETEEN

Friday finds Patrick, myself, and a small entourage (including Sir Dylan, who refuses to leave my side) in Dublin at the Leinster House, where I am told that the Irish Parliament is held. We are admitted and taken to a large room where we are introduced to the president, the prime minister, the council of state and two archbishops of Ireland. The president stands up and begins to speak, "The governing forces of this country have decided that all of the strange circumstances surrounding your presence in our beloved country are most unusual and to some degree suspicious; specifically, your actions at Meath." A rumble of thunder is heard. "It was determined that for now, you, Ms. Connors, will be named 'Honorary Princess of Ireland' until we can thoroughly investigate this situation."

Now, it appears that all hell is breaking lose. There is ongoing thunder and lightning striking all around the Leinster House as well as a deluge of rain. The power goes out, and it seems like the whole building is shaking. Another oddity is that the projection screen in the front of the room rolls down and everyone can see that the only place experiencing this severe weather is the Leinster House!

The president, prime minister, the archbishops, and the council members huddle for a hurried conference. The president clears his throat then says very loudly and clearly, "It appears that the consensus has decided that you truly are the rightful queen of Ireland, and we shall make an official announcement post haste!"

The power comes back on; the lightning mysteriously is gone, but we still hear some rolling thunder. One of the archbishops speaks. "Your majesty, as God is our witness, you will need to have an official coronation ceremony. We hope you will agree to have it here in St. Patrick's Cathedral—if that is acceptable to your ancestors, of course."

"Gentlemen, I am pleased to accept your proposal as it appears that I, too, am at the service of my ancestors—even before I was crowned at the Hill of Tara, after being crowned at the Rock.

"Oh, I almost forgot. I had hoped that the National Historian would be here—Sir Patrick, please." He hands me the parchment that we received. "Upon my return from Meath, there was a visitation at my cottage. I was left with some jewels and this letter, but we require help with its translation, if you would be so kind." I hand the parchment to the archbishop.

"Your majesty, it would be my honor to personally hand this to the historian and send you the translation."

"I thank you, your eminence, you are most kind," I say. "Also at this time I feel I should mention that Sir

Patrick and I are engaged and plan on marrying shortly at the Rock of Cashel."

"But your majesty . . ." the archbishop begins.

"Truly, your majesty, the entire country will be interested in witnessing your union," the president proclaims.

"I understand, gentlemen, and we do so hope that you will also comprehend our desire for privacy. I am sure you all realize that Sir Patrick and I will have little of it upon my coronation. I also expect you will appreciate the outlandish expenditures we are saving the country by keeping this private."

"Oh, yes, yes, that is something to think about," replies the prime minister. There is a boom of thunder, and the gentlemen jump. "We are arranging for your majesty's monthly stipend as we speak."

"We are also placing a royal apartment at your disposal in Dublin Castle," mentions a councilman. There's a crack of lightning outside the window. "What did I say?"

The prime minister speaks up. "What he meant to say was that there will be royal apartments in several of the restored castles throughout the country at your service, your majesty, with of course, room for your staff." The sun comes out, and there's the soft sound of the uilleann pipes.

"Well, gentlemen, it seems that the ancestors are appreciative of all of your actions, as are the Queen and I," replies Patrick. "I believe it is time for us to take our leave. If I may, your majesty." Patrick offers me his arm. The prime minister comes over to open the doors and states, "We have arranged a Land Rover Defender for you, your majesty. We hope that it is to your liking. It is waiting for you out front."

"It is ever so thoughtful of you and greatly appreciated, thank you. After the coronation, when I travel, I expect I'll do most of it by train. I will not be a burden on the country, and I consider myself just an ordinary person with some extraordinary ancestors. Bíodh lá maith agat." (Have a good day.) As we go down the steps, I start laughing and say, "Seems like I've learned some Irish or else my ancestors are now affecting my speech."

TWENTY

Following our trip to Dublin, we stay busy organizing our private wedding. Rose suggests that we film it so that it can be broadcast at a later date, thereby allowing our Irish brethren to witness the first Irish royal wedding in centuries. I feel that Rose is someone I need to guide me through the coming events. I ask her if she'll be my PA and tell her that the government is sending me a list of people I may hire and their salaries. She responds that she is very interested in helping and gives me a big hug. Then she jumps back and apologizes as she curtsies.

Laughing, I say, "Please, Rose, don't apologize, and we can all continue as we always have."

"Not really, we can't. You will have to accept that in public people will curtsey and bow to you as that is what people have to do in the presence of a queen." Rose informs me that there will be a lot of things I will have to study up on in regards to protocol, and I'm stunned and annoyed. I didn't ask for this life. I know I love Patrick and want to marry him, but all this royalty stuff is a wee bit much. Dazed, I just stand there contemplating what the opposite of 'wee' is.

Rose is by my side at the cottage as we view wedding gowns on the net, and I immediately fall in love with the vintage Celtic style. It's white Irish lace with an emerald green sash and a blue line running through the middle with a little around the neck and long sleeves—very simple and modest. I know that Ireland is called the Emerald Isle, but blue is the Celtic color, so I'm combining the two. Rose suggests that I use a blue ribbon for the handfasting part of the ceremony. I also get a few other gowns for future events, and we both gasp and point out an emerald gown with gold lace gown and a cape jacket-like—for the coronation! All of a sudden there is humming, and we see sparkles of light flying around the room.

"It seems that the fairies are happy with our choices," I laugh. Rose is awe struck and can only nod her head. "Is this the first time you've seen the little ones?" Again, she nods her head. "They are mesmerizingly beautiful, aren't they?"

I've asked Ole Annie, Rose, and Bevin to be my bridesmaids, and Patrick is having Finn, Liam and Antonio stand with him so our numbers are by threes and I think St. Pat will be happy with that. Ole Annie has gotten the bishop on board, and the Rock of Cashel's committee is closing the Rock to the public for our ceremony. Ole Annie has given me a white linen handkerchief embroidered with green shamrocks and a horseshoe which I'm to carry open side up. Oh, also I've got to have little bells tied in my bouquet. There seem to be certain Irish traditions that I love learning about and complying with. They tie me to this beautiful land.

Patrick and his groomsmen are wearing their traditional Celtic kilts. They have lavender boutonnieres.

Bevin, Liam, and Antonio are coordinating the reception. Everything is coming together exceptionally well. Patrick has invited Megan and Quinn, not only to the wedding but to stay the night at his pub. Next Sunday is the wedding—Patrick's and my wedding!

TWENTY ONE

It is a beautiful day on Sunday, bright and sunny with a light breeze. It seems like the fairies are around me, flitting and sparkling all the way to the Rock. The committee members have somehow gotten hold of a lovely forest green carpet. Rose and Bevin are in green gowns, and Ole Annie is in a deep blue. There was a bouquet in front of my door this morning with those unique green and yellow roses tied with green and blue ribbons, which are adorned with tiny gold bells that tinkle as I walk. Ole Annie hands me the handkerchief along with the horseshoe. I hear the sweet sound of the uilleann pipes and what sounds like a harp; all provided by my ancestors, or so it seems.

I see Patrick and he's staring at me with a huge smile. I feel the pull between us—this was meant to be! The mass is lovely, and the music never really stops, nor the fairies flitting around the two of us. Sir Dylan is carrying our rings—Claddagh rings for both of us, and Patrick included a diamond band for me as well. After the bishop pronounces us husband and wife and we turn to leave, everyone starts ringing small bells. Paz is flying above us, and as we step outside, we hear the cathedral bells ringing and there is a brilliant rainbow in the sunny sky. The fairies depart, but the mystical music is loud and clear.

Everyone surrounds us and gives us hugs and kisses. Antonio and Bevin come up and say, "Prepare to be surprised." I have no idea what they are talking about, but when we reach the town, we see that it is all adorned in flowers and long tables that are set outside. All the townspeople are here to celebrate us! This is such a special place, and these people so loving, kind, and generous. Long live Eire!

EPILOGUE

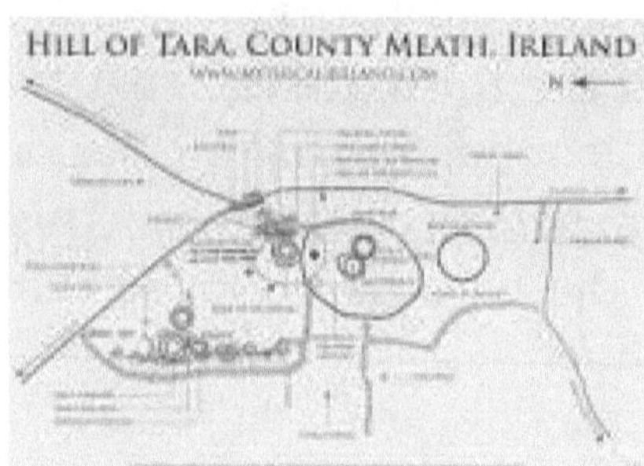

It's six months before the coronation, and I'm not sure that I will be able to learn everything I'm supposed to know. I'm sure that children born into royalty start learning how to act and what to say and do almost before they can speak. Rose has quit her job and is now my personal assistant. Patrick and I have rented a house in town as an office space, and there are days that the phone never stops ringing, nor does the correspondence stop coming. Rose, Patrick, and I reviewed and edited the video of our wedding and put it on a website that Rose set up, and it's been viewed by millions. She also sent it to the three Irish television channels that were grateful for our thoughtfulness.

Patrick and I escape to the Queen's Cottage as soon as we can every night. Our love only seems to grow and a rumor has started that our little cottage glows. Some say that they have seen colorful mists swirling around it. I'm not surprised as I have felt breezes around me that seem like hugs; they make me feel warm and loved. Moonbeam has led us to some hidden jewels in the forest, and Sir Dylan has dug up more. Caramel and Truffle have shown us more secret niches in the cottage as well. It seems that I now have many ancient crown jewels to wear at formal affairs.

At the coronation, Patrick will be named King Consort, and we both are working on our speeches. I'm told that I'll also address the Parliament, and so both Patrick and I are studying all that politics entails. I am so not political and neither is Patrick, so both of us will beseech and invite our leaders to think first about the everyday citizens of Ireland and to stop all hypocritical, fraudulent, and misleading dealings and become the honest, truthful, hardworking leaders that are needed to lead our lovely isle. I know that sounds innocuous, but I am hoping that the majority of the Dail (House of Representatives) and the Seanad (the Senate) will respond well to the invitation.

Something else is strange, as people tell me that I have a very strong Irish accent now and use some old Irish words without knowing it. I've come to accept that Ireland has adopted me, called me home, and loves me. Life is glorious.

IRISH WEDDING TRADITIONS

Traditional Irish wedding customs often involve symbols of luck, love, and commitment, blending ancient Celtic practices with more modern celebrations. Key elements include handfasting, wearing a Claddagh ring, incorporating lucky charms like horseshoes and shamrocks, and enjoying traditional Irish music and dance.

The Claddagh ring

First produced in the 17th century, the design is linked back to the fishing village of Claddagh near Galway. The ring is a symbol of love, friendship and marriage. Claddagh rings are a traditional Irish symbol of love, loyalty, and friendship. The ring features two hands holding a heart, with a crown on top.

Lavender and wild flowers

In an Irish wedding, lavender symbolizes love, devotion, and loyalty. It's often included in the bride's bouquet or headpiece as a symbol of a happy and lasting union. Lavender's calming scent and serene color also contribute to a peaceful atmosphere for the celebration. *Tara does not wear her crown but an ancient tiara which is embedded in a crown of wildflowers.*

The Groom

The groom often wears a traditional Irish kilt, representing his Irish heritage. Irish kilt tartans represent the counties and districts of Ireland. The groom will likely wear a Brian Boru jacket (named for the Irish warrior king), a white tux shirt with bow tie, knee socks with ribbons to match the color of their tartan, a Sporran with shamrock detailing, and Ghillie Brogue shoes.

The handkerchief'

The magic handkerchief is there to symbolize fertility, the bride should have it with her throughout the wedding day, whether it be wrapped in the wedding bouquet or tucked away in her wedding dress. When the wedding is over the magic handkerchief was traditionally kept for the firstborn child and made into a Christening gown. This stunning hand embroidered hankie would be the perfect option if you're following this Irish tradition. *Ole Annie embroidered Tara's with shamrocks.*

Bells

The sound of bells is said to keep away evil spirits, restore harmony and remind a couple of their wedding vows. *Tiny bells were tied onto Tara's bouquet. The wedding guests were also given bells to ring when the ceremony ended.*

Horseshoe

A symbol of good luck, the lucky horseshoe should be displayed pointing up to prevent the luck from running out.

Irish Music and Dance

A lively atmosphere with traditional music like Uilleann pipes and Celtic harps is often part of an Irish wedding. *Tara's ancestors provided the mystical music for her wedding.*

Handfasting

This is where the phrase 'tying the knot' originated from. Handfasting is an ancient Celtic tradition where the couple come together at the beginning of their marriage and hold right hand to right hand then left hand to left hand with their wrists crossed over and the handfasting ribbon is wound around their wrists and over their hands. Handfasting is an ancient Celtic tradition that involves tying the hands of the bride and groom together with a ribbon or cord. This symbolizes their union and commitment to each other. *Rose suggests a blue Celtic knotted ribbon for the handfasting. Blue was also considered lucky for brides, as it was the color of fidelity and symbolized the bride's commitment to their partner.*

9 781966 607250